Y0-BRF-467

The Lion and the Mouse

retold by Cynthia Rothman
illustrated by Thomas Taylor

Table of Contents

Lion and Mouse Meet

One day Lion closed his eyes.
He wanted to fall asleep.

Then, Mouse came by.
Lion heard Mouse
and woke up.

Lion stretched out his paw.
He glared. Then he grabbed
the little mouse.

Mouse began to shake.
He didn't want to fall.

"Great Lion, let me go!"
said Mouse.

A Good Friend

"Why should I let you go?" asked Lion.

Mouse said, "I am just
a little mouse. But I can
be a good friend to you."

"How could a silly little mouse be a friend to me?" asked Lion.

"You will see," said Mouse.

"Ha! Ha! Ha!" said Lion. "Just go now. You made me happy today."

Lion Needs Help

Days passed by. Then
one day Mouse heard
a great and terrible roar.

"Is that my friend?" Mouse
asked. "Did something happen
to Lion?"

Mouse ran in haste.

Before long, Mouse saw what had happened. Lion was trapped in a big net.

"I will help you," Mouse told Lion.

11

"You want to help, but you are so little," Lion said.

"But I can help," said Mouse. "Be still," he told Lion.

Mouse began to nibble at
the net. He made a little hole.

Before long, the hole
grew bigger and bigger.
And soon Lion was free.

Lion was so happy. "Hop on my back," he said. "We will ride together."

And from that day to this, Lion and Mouse are still very good friends.

Comprehension Check

Retell the Story

Use the Beginning, Middle, and End Chart to retell the story.

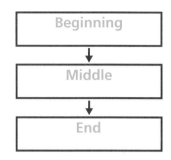

Think and Compare

1. What problem did Mouse have at the beginning of the story? How did he solve it?

2. This book tells how Mouse and Lion became friends. Think about one of your friends. How did you become friends?

3. Mouse helped his friend Lion. How do people who are friends help each other?